This ELMER book belongs to:

. . . .

ELMER'S
TREASURY

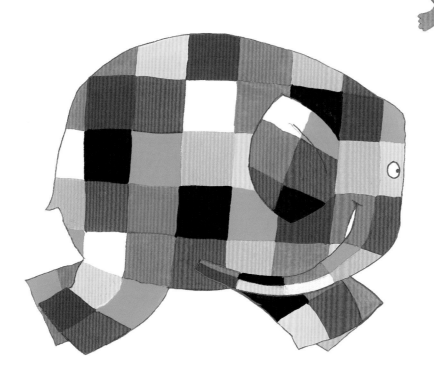

David McKee

ANDERSEN PRESS

First published in Great Britain in 2014 by Andersen Press Ltd.,
20 Vauxhall Bridge Road, London SW1V 2SA.
Published in Australia by Random House Australia Pty.,
Level 3, 100 Pacific Highway, North Sydney, NSW 2060.
Copyright © David McKee, 1989, 1999, 2001, 2005, 2011.
This compilation copyright © David McKee 2014.
The rights of David McKee to be identified as the author and illustrator
of this work have been asserted by him in accordance with the
Copyright, Designs and Patents Act, 1988.
All rights reserved.
Colour separated in Switzerland by Photolitho AG, Zürich.
Printed and bound in China by C&C Offset Printing Co., Ltd.

10   9   8   7   6   5   4   3   2   1

British Library Cataloguing in Publication Data available.

ISBN 978 1 78344 180 8

CONTENTS

ELMER

There was once a herd of elephants. Elephants
young, elephants old, elephants tall or fat or thin.
Elephants like this, that or the other, all different but all
happy and all the same colour. All, that is, except Elmer.

14

Elmer was different. Elmer was patchwork.
Elmer was yellow and orange
and red and pink and purple
and blue and green
and black and white.

Elmer was *not* elephant colour.

It was Elmer who kept the elephants happy. Sometimes he joked with the other elephants, sometimes they joked with him. But if there was even a little smile, it was usually Elmer who started it.

One night Elmer couldn't sleep for thinking, and the think that he was thinking was that he was tired of being different. "Whoever heard of a patchwork elephant?" he thought. "No wonder they laugh at me."

In the morning before the others were really awake, Elmer slipped quietly away, unnoticed.

As he walked through the jungle, Elmer met other animals.

They always said: "Good morning, Elmer." Each time,
Elmer smiled and said: "Good morning."

After a long walk, Elmer found what he was looking for – a large bush. A large bush covered with berries, a large bush covered with elephant-coloured berries. Elmer caught hold of the bush and shook it and shook it so that the berries fell on the ground.

Once the ground was covered in berries, Elmer lay down and rolled over and over – this way and that way and back again. Then he picked up bunches of berries and rubbed himself all over, covering himself with berry juice until there wasn't a sign of any yellow, or orange, or red, or pink, or purple, or blue, or green, or black, or white.

When he had finished, Elmer looked like any other elephant.

After that Elmer set off back to the herd.
On the way, he passed the other animals again.

This time each one said to him: "Good morning,
elephant." And each time Elmer smiled and said:
"Good morning," pleased that he wasn't recognised.

When Elmer rejoined the other elephants, they were all standing quietly. None of them noticed Elmer as he worked his way to the middle of the herd.

After a while Elmer felt that something was wrong. But what? He looked around: same old jungle, same old bright sky, same old rain cloud that came over from time to time and lastly same old elephants. Elmer looked at them.

The elephants were standing absolutely still.
Elmer had never seen them so serious before.
The more he looked at the serious, silent, still,

standing elephants, the more he wanted to laugh.
Finally he could bear it no longer.
He lifted his trunk and at the top of his voice shouted:

The elephants jumped and fell all ways in surprise.
"Oh my gosh and golly!" they said –
and then saw Elmer, helpless with laughter.

"Elmer," they said. "It must be Elmer."
Then the other elephants laughed too,
as they had never laughed before.

37

As they laughed, the rain cloud burst and when the rain fell on Elmer, his patchwork started to show again. The elephants still laughed as Elmer was washed back to normal. "Oh Elmer," gasped an old elephant. "You've played some good jokes, but this has been the

biggest laugh of all. It didn't take you long to show your true colours."

"We must celebrate this day every year," said another. "This will be Elmer's Day. All elephants must decorate themselves and Elmer will decorate himself elephant colour."

That is exactly what the elephants do.
On one day a year they decorate themselves and parade.
On that day if you happen to see an elephant ordinary
elephant colour, you will know it must be Elmer.

ELMER
and the LOST TEDDY

The sky was already dark and full of stars when Elmer,
the patchwork elephant, heard the sound of crying.
It was Baby Elephant.
"He can't sleep," said Baby Elephant's mother.
"He wants his teddy. We took Teddy with us on a
picnic and somewhere we lost it."

"Never mind," said Elmer.
"I'll lend him my teddy. Tomorrow I'll
look for the lost one."
Elmer went away and came back with his
teddy. Baby Elephant smiled and was soon
fast asleep with Elmer's teddy beside him.

The next day Elmer set off in search of the lost teddy. He hadn't gone far when he met his cousin, Wilbur. "Hello, Wilbur," said Elmer. "I'm looking for Baby Elephant's lost teddy. Have you seen it?" "No," said Wilbur. "But if I find it, I'll call you."

A little later a voice said, "Hello, Elmer. Where are you going?" It was Lion.

"Baby Elephant has lost his teddy and I'm looking for it," said Elmer.

"Oh dear," said Lion. "Baby Lion would be very upset if he lost his teddy. If I find it, I'll call you. Maybe Tiger has seen it."

As he came near Tiger's place, Elmer called out, "Yoho! Tiger!"
"Ssssh! Elmer," Tiger quietly called back. "The twins
are asleep."
"Sorry," said Elmer. "Only, Baby Elephant has lost his
teddy. Have you seen it?"
"That's serious," said Tiger. "The twins wouldn't
sleep without their teddies. If I find it, I'll call you."

After that, Elmer visited the other animals.
All the young ones had their teddies, but
none of them had seen Baby Elephant's.
They all said the same thing, "If we find
it, we'll call you."

It was getting late into the afternoon and Teddy was still lost. "I hope I find him soon," thought Elmer. "It's nearly night-time." It was at that moment that he heard a shout. "Help! Help!" And then again: "Help! I'm lost!"

Elmer pushed through some bushes and there
was a teddy bear. The voice came from the teddy.
"Please help me," said the teddy. "I'm lost. I want
Baby Elephant."
"You can talk," said Elmer in surprise.
"Please, take me home," said Teddy. "I can't
sleep without Baby Elephant."

Elmer still stared. "Your mouth isn't moving," he said.
Just then Wilbur appeared from the bushes.

"Wilbur," laughed Elmer. "I might have known it was you making Teddy speak."

Wilbur chuckled. "I said I'd call you if I found Teddy," he said. "And I did. Come on, let's take Teddy home, it's getting dark."

They set off together,
singing as they went.

Baby Elephant was excited to see his teddy
again and quickly gave back Elmer's teddy.

Baby Elephant's mother couldn't
thank Elmer and Wilbur enough.   65

"Elmer," said Wilbur, "weren't you worried that Baby Elephant would want to keep your teddy? Your teddy is very different; it's special."

"But, Wilbur, didn't you know?" said Elmer in surprise. "You don't have to be different to be special. All teddies are special, especially your own."

ELMER

and GRANDPA ELDO

Elmer, the patchwork elephant, was picking fruit.
"Picking fruit, Elmer?" asked a monkey.
"I'm going to see Grandpa Eldo and this is his
favourite," said Elmer.
"Golden Grandpa Eldo," said Monkey. "That's nice."

Grandpa Eldo was pleased to see Elmer.
"What a lovely surprise," he said.
"What's that balanced on your head?"

"Your favourite fruit," said Elmer.
"Fancy you remembering that," said Eldo.
"I remember lots of things," said Elmer.

"What else do you remember?" asked Eldo.
"The walks we used to go on," said Elmer.
"Walks? Where did we go?" Eldo asked.
"Don't you remember?" said Elmer. "I'll
show you. Come on."

"We used to come this way, past the rocks," said Elmer.
"Here I used to hide, then jump out and shout . . ."
Elmer turned around, but Eldo wasn't there. "Grandpa?
Grandpa Eldo, where are you?" he called.

Eldo suddenly jumped out in front of Elmer.
"BOO!" he shouted.
"Oh, Grandpa!" Elmer laughed. "I was supposed to
do that. Come on, now we go down to the stream." 79

At the stream Elmer said, "Don't you remember anything? We used to play stepping stones."
"Show me," said Eldo.

There were already some rocks in the water. Elmer added more to fill in the spaces. "Now walk across," he said. "Be careful, there's usually a wobbly one."

Suddenly there was a huge splash! Elmer had fallen in.
"You were right. You've a good memory," Eldo chuckled.
Elmer laughed. "Lucky it's not deep."
"Now where?" asked Eldo.
"You still don't remember," said Elmer. "To the lake,
of course."

"We used to play Ducks and Drakes," said Elmer. He picked up a flat stone and sent it skipping across the water. "Seven splashes," he said.

"Let me try," said Eldo.

"You need a nice flat stone," said Elmer, but Eldo had already thrown. "1, 2, 3, 4, 5, 6, 7, 8, 9," they counted together.

When they set off again, Elmer started to sing. Eldo joined in, then the birds joined in too.

"When we're marching on our way,
bumpity bump, bumpity bump.
We like to laugh and play,
bumpity bump, bumpity bump.
And when we can't think what to do
We simply hide and then shout, 'BOOOOO!'
When we're marching on our way,
bumpity bump, bumpity bump!"

When they shouted, "BOO!" the birds flew around squawking with laughter.

It started to rain and they dashed into a cave for shelter. "Surely you remember the stories you used to tell me?" Elmer asked.

Eldo frowned. "What were they?" he asked.

"*Red Riding Hood, Jack and the Beanstalk, Cinderella, Three Little Pigs* . . . Mmmm . . . *Billygoats Gruff* . . . Aaaah . . . *Sleeping Beauty* . . ." Elmer hesitated.

"*Hansel and Gretel, Tom Thumb, Goldilocks* . . ." Eldo continued.

"You cheat, you do remember!" said Elmer.

Eldo laughed and, now the rain had stopped,
ran off. Elmer chased him all the way back to Eldo's
place shouting, "You tricked me. You remembered
everything. I'll get you, Grandpa Eldo."

90

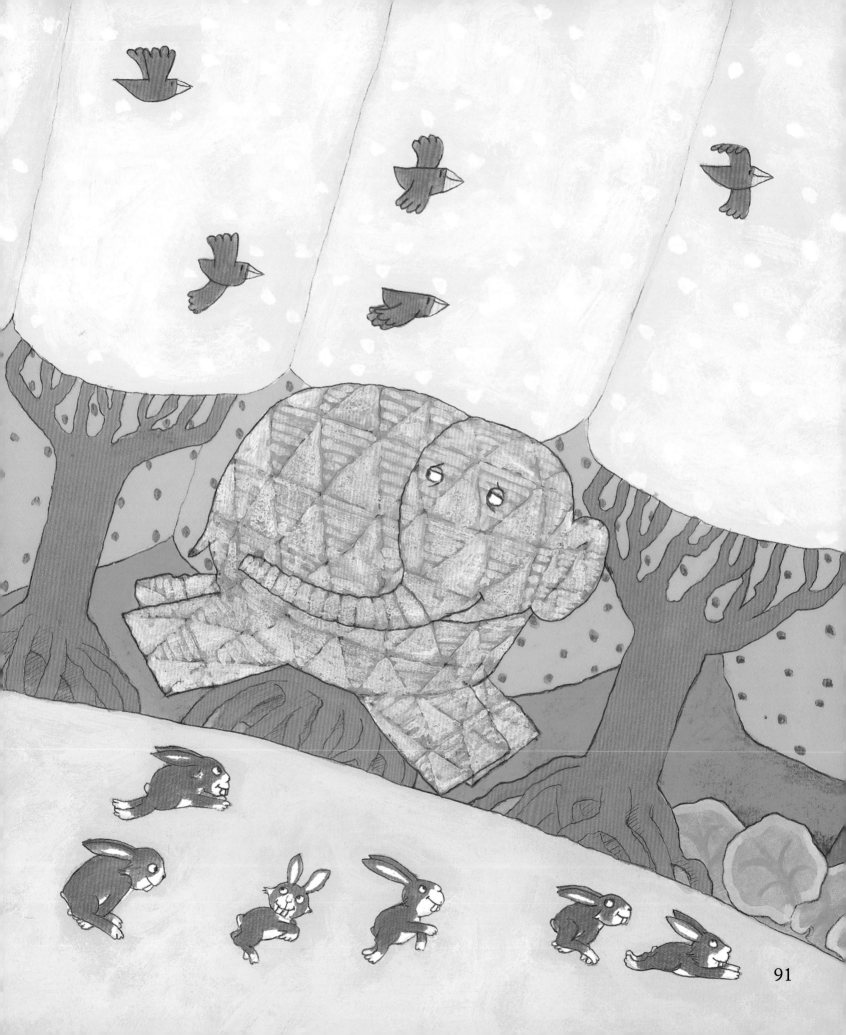

After they had their breath back, and stopped laughing, and finished the fruit that Elmer had brought, it was time to go home.

"It's been fun, Grandpa," said Elmer. "You really remembered everything, didn't you?"

"Yes," chuckled Eldo, "and I was so happy that you did, too. But best of all, you remembered to visit me."

Elmer smiled, "Bye, Grandpa," he said. "See you soon."

ELMER
and SUPER EL

Elmer, the patchwork elephant, was taking his morning walk when he heard an "Oh no!" Looking round, he spotted a small elephant dressed in an outfit that he recognised.

"Hello, Super El," Elmer said with a smile. "What's the problem?"

"Look," said the small elephant, showing his torn outfit. "That thorn bush attacked me! If I'm seen like this, I'll be laughed at. That's not very super."

"Aunt Zelda will soon fix that," said Elmer. "We'll just have to make sure that you're not seen. Our first problem will be to pass the elephants. I'll distract them. Come on. It will be fun!"

Elmer went to the elephants and called out,
"I've just heard a good joke, listen."
The elephants all looked at him.
"There was an elephant, a lion and a fish . . ."
he began. "Oh dear, I've forgotten the rest!"
"That's a good one," the elephants laughed.
"Elephants never forget!"
Meanwhile Super El slipped past unnoticed.

Elmer and Super El hadn't gone far when they heard
Lion and Tiger approaching. "Hello," said Elmer.
"Nice day for it."

"Eh? What?" asked Lion and Tiger together. They were confused enough not to notice the little elephant on the rocks above them.

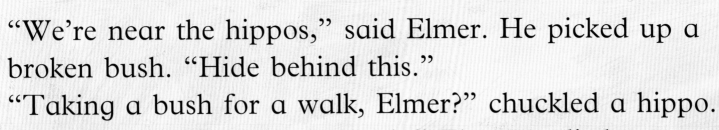

"We're near the hippos," said Elmer. He picked up a broken bush. "Hide behind this."
"Taking a bush for a walk, Elmer?" chuckled a hippo.
"There's an elephant behind it," Elmer replied.
"Always joking, Elmer," the hippos laughed.
Once they were safely past, Elmer said, "Wait here, Super El. I've an idea how we can get past both Snake and the rabbits."

The rabbits were listening enthralled to
Snake, as the two elephants slipped past them.
"What's going on?" asked Super El.
"I asked Snake to tell the rabbits about the time
he tricked me and the elephants," said Elmer.
"He tells it beautifully. They haven't noticed us."

When they came to the crocodiles, Elmer threw a branch into the river to distract them. Then he and Super El crossed in the confusion that followed.

"It's not going to be easy to pass the monkeys," said Elmer.
"Leave that to us," said the birds.

The birds were wonderful. They sang and flew in patterns above the monkeys' heads. The monkeys were too fascinated to notice the elephants. The little elephant nearly stopped to watch, but Elmer pushed him along.

"Thanks, birds," said Elmer later. "You were fantastic! Look, there's Aunt Zelda saying goodbye to some friends. As soon as they've left, we'll go to her. Remember, she doesn't always hear too well."

112

When the others had gone, Elmer said, "Hello, Aunt Zelda, this is my friend Super El."
"Yes, I'm very well, thank you, Elmer dear," said Aunt Zelda. "But your friend's suit looks in a bit of a state. Shall I mend it?"
"Oh, yes please!" said the little elephant.

"Aunt Zelda," said Elmer, "you are a wonder."
"Thunder, dear? I didn't hear anything," said
Aunt Zelda.
Super El smiled, and Aunt Zelda quickly
finished the repairs.

"Thank you, now I feel super again," said the little elephant. "I think you're both wonderful. Maybe one day I can do something for you."
With that, he shot off like a rocket into the sky.
He looped back just once to wave goodbye.
"If he's going to rush about like that he'll spoil his clothes again," said Aunt Zelda.
"Probably," said Elmer, chuckling. "Probably."

ELMER
and ROSE

A young friend of Elmer's named Rose
Blushes from her head to her toes,
Or sometimes instead
From her toes to her head
But never from her tail to her nose.

Elmer, the patchwork elephant, was with his cousin
Wilbur. They were looking at the herd of elephants.
"Jolly fellows," smiled Wilbur, "but not exactly unique."
"They're all unique," said Elmer. "Just not as different
as us. Imagine a herd like you or me."

At that moment Bird arrived and said,
"Grandpa Eldo wants you two."
"Come on, Wilbur," said Elmer.

126

Grandpa Eldo was looking under a bush.
"Where is she?" he muttered.
Then, seeing Elmer and Wilbur, he said,
"She must be hiding from you two."
"She?" said Elmer. "Who are you
talking about?"

"Rose," said Eldo. "She wandered away from a herd of elephants that passed nearby. You two can take her back to them. Ah! There she is. Don't be frightened, Rose. Come and meet Elmer and Wilbur."

From behind a tree peeped a young elephant: a pink elephant.

131

"Oh!" said Elmer and Wilbur in surprise.
"Very pretty," Elmer added quickly.
Rose became even pinker.
"She blushes very easily," whispered Eldo.
"I expect that's why she's called 'Rose'."
Rose said, "Pleased to
meet you," and
blushed again.

"You'll find the tracks of the herd by the lake, just follow them," said Eldo. "You'll go faster than I would. Goodbye, Rose."
Rose said, "goodbye" very sweetly, blushed a deeper pink and ran after Elmer and Wilbur.

At the lake they met another elephant.
Rose stared and hid between Elmer and Wilbur.
"Hello, Elmer. Hello, Wilbur," said the elephant.
"Hello . . ." he continued awkwardly, looking at Rose.
"Rose," said Elmer helpfully.
After the elephant had gone, Rose said,
"That's a strange one."

Every so often, to make the journey more fun,
they raced each other.

Rose loved that because somehow she always won,
and every time she blushed even pinker.

Between races Wilbur played tricks with his voice.
He made his voice roar from behind a rock and shout
from a treetop. Rose squealed with excitement, blushed
almost red and held on to Elmer's trunk.
Elmer just chuckled.

Suddenly Rose said excitedly, "Listen!
They're just over the hill. I'll go alone now.
You may upset the others, they're quite shy.
You're all such unusual elephants, especially
the strange grey one we saw. Thank you for
bringing me back."
"Come and visit us sometime," Elmer called after her.
"Strange grey one? What did she mean?" asked Wilbur.
"I think she was joking," said Elmer.

From the hill they watched Rose safely
join the herd.
"She wasn't joking," said Elmer.
"No wonder she found the grey
elephant strange."

The elephants in Rose's herd were all . . .

PINK!

Going home, Elmer and Wilbur were met by Eldo. "You knew about the pink elephants, didn't you, Grandpa Eldo?" said Elmer.

"Yes, I wanted you to see them," said Eldo.

"Rose was nice," said Wilbur. "I thought she was unique, and she thought the grey elephant was unique."

"They're probably all nice, unique or not," said Elmer.

Wilbur grinned. "Remember what you
said, Elmer. Imagine a herd like one of us."
"Especially like you, Elmer," laughed Eldo.
Elmer smiled and said nothing.
He was imagining a herd of
elephants like himself . . .

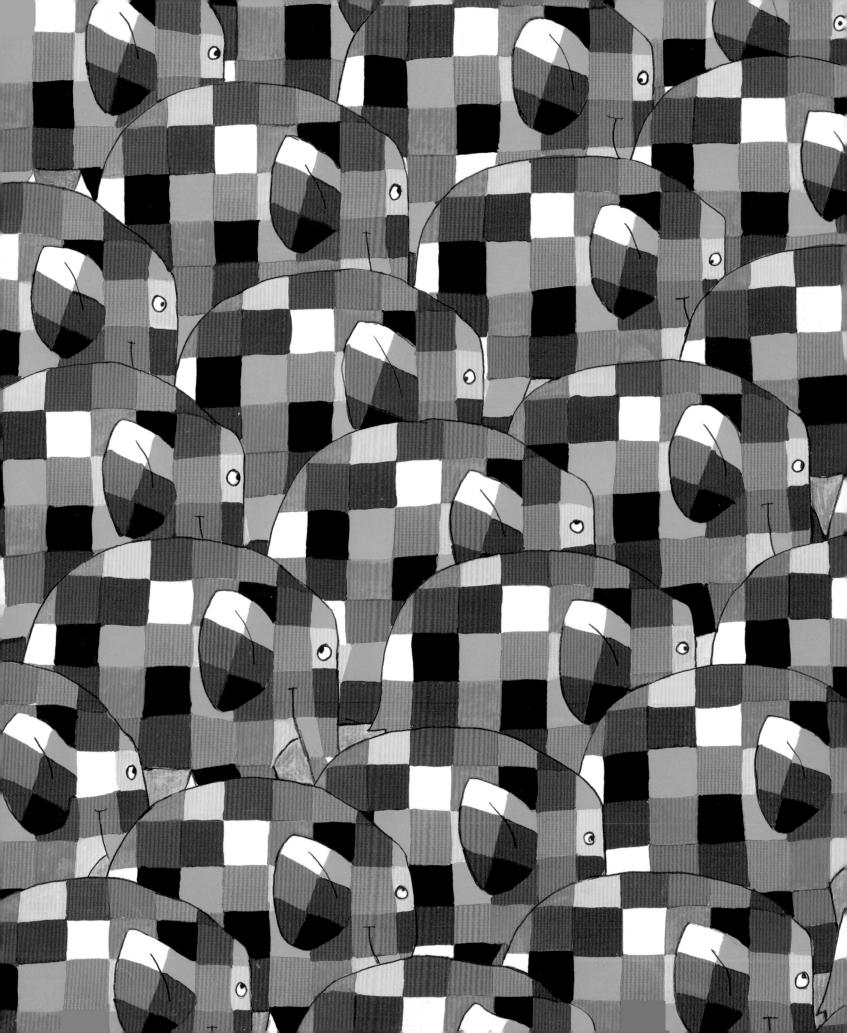